for my
mam
+
dad
I love you

First published in Great Britain in 2003 by Brimax™,
an imprint of Octopus Publishing Group Ltd
2-4 Heron Quays, London E14 4JP

A CIP catalogue record for this book is available
from the British Library.

ISBN 1 85854 612 5 (hardback)
ISBN 1 85854 703 2 (paperback)

Printed in China

This **longs to :**

● ●

Pirate Jam

by **Jo Brown**

BRIMAX

Once upon a time, in the middle of the deep blue sea, lived a gang of pirates. As there were only two of them, you couldn't call them a gang at all - maybe just a pair of pirates.

Their names were Fredbeard and Little Jim.
Fredbeard's friends called him Fred,
and Jim wasn't little at all. (Well, he was once.)
They had a little sea dog called Patch.

Fred and Little Jim weren't fierce pirates at all.
They were thrown out of pirate school because
they had failed all their exams.
"You two be useless pirates!" said their teacher.

They'd rather have
a cup of tea than
a bottle of grog.

They couldn't
buckle swashes.

And they always held treasure
maps the wrong way up.

Little Jim and Fred had
no idea how to splice a
mainbrace or hoist sails.

They found shivering timbers a bit of a bore
and they always got seasick.

Instead of making someone walk the plank,
they'd rather walk the dog. (Which suited Patch fine.)

After leaving pirate school, Fred and Little Jim
sailed around for a while until they spotted
the perfect island to make their home.

They built a little house from driftwood and other things
they found on the beach. In the garden they built a shed,
where Fred stored anything he thought might be useful.
Little Jim tried to keep it tidy.

Once they'd settled in, Fred and Little Jim needed something to do. They wanted to be useful pirates.

Little Jim tried gardening, but Fred had buried treasure in the vegetable patch, so there wasn't much room for anything else. Slugs ate all of their lettuce, the tomatoes wouldn't ripen, and the strawberries went all mushy.

Fred tried being a postman, but he got everything muddled up because he held the map the wrong way up.

He delivered the right letters to the wrong people.

He squashed parcels (especially the ones marked "Do Not Squash")...

and he delivered birthday cards three days late.

His cutlass was a problem, too. It accidentally tore open packages, and things were always spilling out - like knitting needles, left shoes, and pieces of jigsaw puzzles (usually bits of sky).

Fred collected up all these leftover bits and put them in the shed.

One night, there was a terrible storm. Fred, Little Jim, and Patch were warm and dry in their cosy house. They were very glad that they weren't out at sea like their old friends from pirate school.

The next day, lots of boxes washed up on the shore.
The pirates went to investigate, but they found
no pirate treasure, no gold coins, no yo ho ho and
a bottle of rum. In the boxes were sacks of sugar
and lots of brightly coloured wool.

The pirates gathered up the boxes and stored the salvage in their shed. Fred said it would be useful some day.

**Little Jim looked doubtful but he liked to keep
the beach tidy. There wasn't much room left in the shed.**

One day, Fred and Little Jim were having a nice cup of tea and a slice of toast. "It would be grand if we had something to put on this here toast," said Little Jim.

Then Fred had a bright idea.
(He hadn't had a bright idea before,
so he had to lie down for a while.)

When he got up, Fred picked all the squishy strawberries. Then he went to the shed and found the shipwrecked sugar. He put it all in a big pan on the stove and boiled it up to make jam.

Then he poured it
into jars and drew
his picture on the
labels.

"Ahar! It be Pirate Jam!"

Fred made some more
toast for Little Jim,
this time with jam.

After finishing his toast, Little Jim went to tidy the shed.
He'd almost finished when he spotted the shipwrecked
wool and some knitting needles.
"Hmm," he thought, "Oits getting a bit chilly these days,
maybe I could make us some jumpers."

He remembered how his granny had taught him
to knit years before and set to.

Soon, he had a whole box full of woolly jumpers, socks, and scarves. He showed them to Fred, who had another good idea (he was getting used to it by now). "Let's take our jam and jumpers to the market!"

The market was very busy.

Soon everyone had heard about the delicious strawberry jam and the warm, snuggly jumpers.
By the end of the day, the pirates had sold everything and had a big bag of gold to take home.
(They decided not to bury it in the garden this time.)

Fredbeard and Little Jim had finally proved they were very useful pirates - and they didn't even need to go to sea!